I Know Why
She Swallowed a Fly

* * * * *

Disclaimer

This is a work of fiction, a product of the author's imagination. Any resemblance or similarity to any actual events or persons, living or dead, is purely coincidental.

Formatted by Debora Lewis arenapublishing.org

ISBN-13: 978-1519163103
ISBN-10: 151916310X

I Know Why
She Swallowed a Fly

Colleen Crowlie

Illustrator Burke Richardson

I KNOW WHY SHE SWALLOWED A FLY

The Little Old Lady Who Swallowed a Fly Was My Best Friend and I am outraged that her death is just a big joke to the very men who killed her, those Folk Singers, who lured her into gambling away her life. Just a funny song they sing to make people laugh is how they tell it. But that's not the true story, and I'm going to tell it to you right now because Ida (that was her name in real life) and I were Best Friends for 60 years and she deserves more respect than this silly song.

Sure, it's stupid to swallow a fly. But it's not really that big a deal for a woman raised on a cattle ranch. Cow patties, as my Grandma used to call cow manure, are what flies love best and, on a ranch, everybody ends up with a fly buzzing in the mouth after taking a careless drink. So please, don't act like that killed her. It was the drinking, gambling and sibling rivalry that got her.

But let's not worry about that right now. I want you to know what a great friend she was.

We went to the movies every Saturday. When Betty Boop cartoons came on, she'd pull my pigtails and say, "Boop-oop-a-doop – you're Betty Boop." It made me proud to be a Betty. The best parts of my childhood were the things I did with Ida.

Ida and I liked to climb trees, and we built one of the best tree house forts in the county, until her brothers raided it. They just wrecked things for the fun of it. And they stole all our good stuff. But that made it more exciting because we had to be secretive and steal back our stuff. Then we stole some of their stuff too. The competition in her family was fierce.

We were best friends all through school, but after high school graduation, she went off to college, and became a school teacher, and I stayed home and married a rancher. It wasn't until she came back years later to be the principal of the Rosedale Elementary School that we got close again.

I was the only one she could blow off steam with, and we used to go to Las Vegas and do a little gambling. Maybe not so little, she did have a gambling problem, I have to admit.

She loved playing craps, and her ex says she gambled away his retirement savings. It wasn't that much according to her, a $10,000 savings. Like that was going to change his life.

I was her best friend on the day she died and I'm not going to let this silly song make it look like there was no reason for her to do all that crazy stuff.

I know why she swallowed the fly.

32 ND ANNUAL LAS VEGAS HOOTENANNY

"Perhaps she'll die" is the cold-hearted way you look at the situation, Mister Folksinger. But I say, it was murder, and you're to blame.

You tricked her into swallowing that fly by betting her $50 she wouldn't swallow a fly. You knew what a gambling fool she was; that she'd do anything to win a bet against her brother, your fiddling partner. It's pretty suspicious that you had this whole song to sing after inviting us to the Hootenanny to see your star performance. It was premeditated murder…. "Ha ha ha" is what you say. Well, why don't you just listen to the facts.

11

The fly was weird.

Her brother claims that he caught this weird fly out of the air and, for a lark, bet his Big Sister $50 to eat it. I doubt that, because the close-up picture I took doesn't show an ordinary fly. I think he brought this sucker to the Hootenanny knowing he was going to make a bet and set the Little Old Lady off on the train of betting till she lost it all. She was a nut case that way. Once she started betting and winning she couldn't stop until she lost it all.

And she did win the first $50 bet.

She popped the fly into her mouth and swallowed.

Little Old Lady $100 winner

Double or nothing
The spider was weirder

Her eyes got big and she was gagging, when you yelled out "double or nothing if you swallow a spider." This strange looking spider seemed to appear from nowhere in her brother's hand.

You interpreted the distress sounds from the buzzing in her throat as a yes and her brother threw the spider into her mouth. She swallowed hard.

Then she was up $200 and the lights started flashing and the bells were ringing and a winsome cocktail hostess brought us drinks from an admirer in the audience. And there was her brother plucking his fiddle in the fight way he'd been doing since 5th grade. You, Mister Folksinger, were strumming and singing about the spider that was wiggling and jiggling inside her. It wasn't looking too good for the Old Lady because she was still thinking she was the winner and she would have been if she had taken the $200 for swallowing a fly and a spider.

Little Old Lady $200 winner

Double or nothing. Again.

I begged her not to, but she took the bet. It wasn't absurd that she swallowed the bird, it was enticement by you, Mr. Folksinger, you riled up the crowd cheering her on to swallow the bird. And you are a turd for giving her the bird.

What a show-off the Little Old Lady was. She loved the cheers, "Just do it!" and she did. Making awful squawking noises as she swallowed the bird, but she got it down.

Little Old Lady $400 winner

More gin and tonics, bells and whistles,
spinning colored lights.
Double Dumb is Double or Nothing again. And again

Imagine that, she swallowed a cat. No, I can't imagine that, where did you come up with such an idea? Is there no law in Nevada that protects cats from being fed to old ladies? I can't believe this really happened but I saw it with my own eyes so I know it did.

You kept singing, "perhaps she'll die," after getting her to gulp down each animal, but I was slow to realize that you meant it. And it was after another gin and tonic when she bet her brother she could swallow a cat, and a trucker from Kansas threw a cat down her throat, that I realized you were trying to kill her. Nobody brings a cat to a hootenanny.

But still the Little Old Lady thought she was winning because the screen on stage was flashing $800 – BIG WINNER-LOL

Little Old Lady $800 winner and cruising for a bruising like my dad used to say

Double or Nothing. Again, again, again
Blurry vision, loud voices, I want to go home.

The crowd was going crazy, wanting to see what the Old Lady would swallow next. You could tell she was so confused, having swallowed a cat to catch the bird, and a bird to catch the spider, and a spider to catch the fly, that she didn't think twice about swallowing a dog.

Yes, on stage she swallowed a dog, and you called her a hog for swallowing a dog.

Well I'm calling you a murderer, Mr. Folksinger. You killed a dog just for this silly song and a bet. Sure she was the one that swallowed it, but you had it brought on stage with a leash and then bet her "Double or Nothing, for the $800 to swallow a dog." That's criminal intent or something. Whose dog was that?

Little Old Lady $1600 winner. The cocktail waitresses did a conga line of drinks over to our table. Everyone in the room seemed to be sending us drinks and raising their glasses as the Little Old Lady staggered around the room, raising her hands over her head like a winning fighter.

Double or nothing.... And I can't keep up with the agains.

The Goat, I can't believe the Preacher came with a goat, and you are saying this wasn't premeditated murder, just a good payback joke. I don't think so, enticing a person to open up her throat and swallow a goat is... just crazy and wrong and that Preacher was so bad, I can't believe it happened, but it did.

Her brother waved all those hundred dollar bills in her face singing "I don't know why she swallowed a fly perhaps she'll die," after every animal because he could see how mad it made her.

Oh. A chilly wind blew through the room and I begged her to leave, but when they finally got the doors and windows closed, you, Mr. Folksinger, flashed your 'Double or Nothing' offer at her. She didn't even ask "What for?" She punched her arms in the air and the crowd yelled, "Just do it!" She was three sheets to the wind with a gut full of trouble by then. Should she really have been allowed to bet the $1600?

"No! No! No!" I screamed, but somehow she managed to swallow the goat. Everybody that saw sat back in awe.

She just opened up her throat and swallowed a goat? It took that Trucker and his 3 friends to get that goat down her throat.

Little Old Lady $3200 winner

Double or nothing is a crazy game but my friend won't see it.

Of course, her ex husband brought the cow; I don't know how he knew to bring a cow to a Hootenanny or why she bet him she could swallow it. But she always did find fighting with him inspiring.

That cow was so dumb that she just let the ex husband walk her into the Old Lady's mouth which was easy to do since the Old Lady had fallen to the floor. The Little Old Lady wasn't little after swallowing the cow. She was HUGE AND A BIG WINNER with every light and bell in the casino going off, celebrating this incredible win. The crowd was going crazy. They had to call extra security to keep her fans back. And still you didn't stop singing this ridiculous song predicting her death. "Perhaps she'll die!!!!!!!" Of course she'll die if she keeps eating.

Huge Old Lady $6400 winner

27

Double or nothing and you are a loser even if you win.

It is unconscionable that as the Huge Old Lady was rolling around on the floor with a cow in her belly that you interpreted the kicking of her legs as accepting your DOUBLE OR NOTHING offer. I think if you look at the security tapes, you will see that this was a person in distress, not a woman placing a bet.

But her brother brought out the horse, and, in her distress over the cow kicking around in her stomach, she swallowed the horse. And all you can say is, "She died of course."

Dead Old Lady $12,800 winner
She paid for her own funeral

Mr. Folksinger, it's not right to be encouraging people to laugh at the way she died. She was a good old gal who wasn't afraid to eat a little fly on a bet. She was the only girl in her family with three older brothers and one younger. She was tough from fighting her older brothers and bullying her little one. When she was the principal of Rosedale Elementary, they called her the Iron Lady. Who would have thought her youngest brother would be the one to do her in, betting her to swallow a horse?

It took him 60 years to best her. He knew what a show-off she was, and he knew how to stir up the crowd, so she wanted to be all tough for them. Acting like it was important to take every bet because people were cheering her on; she just loved that sound. How mean of him getting his big sister to keep making those crazy bets.

Yeah, she had been kind of mean, especially to her younger brother. Every mean thing her older brothers did to her, she tried them on her younger brother. And I laughed every time.

I guess people don't change much. Ida was always a wild one.

I met her in kindergarten. She had a real donkey and she would smear molasses on her little brother's face, and tie him to a post, and let the donkey lick it off his face. He would scrunch and wriggle as the big donkey tongue keep licking and licking every drop of molasses. He looked so ridiculous even their Mom laughed.

So sure, I understand how her little brother had issues with his big sister. But I was shocked when he got the preacher to bring in the goat.... A man of God asking someone to open up her throat to swallow a goat.

I guess he was getting even for that Mother's Day, long ago, when the Little Old Lady put a goat wearing the preacher's coat in the church. The goat climbed in the choir to eat the corsages off the singers, smacking his goat lips on the pins and butting a woman who wouldn't let go of her flower. Watching the preacher running around in his shirtsleeves, trying to get the goat out, we laughed until we cried. It's my happiest Mother's Day memory.

The Little Old Lady had done that 30 years ago, but I guess the preacher still hadn't forgiven her trespasses and owed her a goat, down her throat.

RIP

L ITTLE
O LD
L ADY

Then she ate that cow and hadn't even gotten her mouth shut when her brother Andy comes with a horse and has it jump in her mouth. She died, of course.

Yes, of course, she died. You killed her, Mr. Folksinger.

I think they should have charged you with her death. Yes, you did make her famous. She always said she was going to be famous, more famous than anybody we ever knew. And now she is. Everybody knows the Little Old Lady who swallowed a fly, and now you know the true story of how it really happened. I guess that's justice enough for me.

There is no fool like an old fool, but she was my Best Friend and I'm kind of proud of how she can still make us laugh. She did die, but maybe it was for a good cause.

Sing on Mr. Folksinger.

I was the
Little Old Lady's (who swallowed a fly)
Best Friend

ABOUT THE AUTHOR

Colleen Crowlie is a storyteller who has sung this song dozens of times and wondered, why did the Old Lady swallow a fly and all those other animals. It's funny, but why? After much research and investigation, Colleen discovered Betty's story, which unfortunately does not seem to be destined for the Elementary School Library market. That's the problem with true stories about Old Ladies.

But many of the Old Lady's fans are grown now and they'll understand and appreciate the details of the Old Lady's crazy behavior. Isn't that what we love to read about as adults–other people's bad behavior, especially famous people, like the Little Old Lady Who Swallowed a Fly.

Her first book *Step by Step: Beautiful Bisbee ~ Plants* is a winner in the Gardening category of the 2015 New Mexico-Arizona Book Awards. Co- author Cado Daily showed Colleen the joy of collaboration and how much better a book turns out with a joint effort So Colleen has gone on to collaborate with Burke Richardson whose humor and love light up these pages.

ABOUT THE ILLUSTRATOR

Burke Richardson was an Air Force brat whose family eventually settled in St. Louis, and he is now a Spanish speaker living on the Mexican Border. He has lived in Bisbee for eighteen years and has captured Bisbee's funky lifestyle with his humorous postcards.

He and artist/architect Todd Bogatay ran the Spirit Gallery on Tombstone Canyon for many years. In addition to showcasing local visual artists, it served as a meeting place for creative people of all types, from comedians to poets.

He is now living on the edge, working on everything from book illustrations to remodeling. Sea monsters and the trashy story of Old McDonald's Farm are the book projects his is working on.

An animal lover and a jokester, Burke was the perfect artist to illustrate this this book. His characters have so much personality you know you are seeing the real deal.